Bondage Beta-Tester - BDSM Enhancement Upgrade . . . Inevitable

BONDAGE BETA-TESTS, Volume 1

Zatanna Dark

Published by Zatanna Dark, 2022.

BONDAGE BETA-TESTER - BDSM ENHANCEMENT UPGRADE … INEVITABLE

First edition. March 23, 2022.

ISBN: 979-8227626295

Written by Zatanna Dark.

Table of Contents

SUSPENSE...

The human body is an amazing thing, but I don't think it was designed to be suspended and tortured twelve or more hours at a time. Designed that way or not, I don't have any choice but to endure the results of the path and decisions I've made.

Strapped, locked and being held in mid air as ongoing shocks of electro stimulation ravage my body. I shake, shiver, spasm as the pain and pleasure confuses me as I enter another uncontrollable extra long orgasm as I scream again into my gag.

Once I was put into this predicament, the Dream Mistress of my own making has left me to suffer in pleasure . . . I'm alone and helpless . . . even though I'm being watched and monitored from a distance.

Problem is, these watchers don't care if I'm suffering or am begging them with my eyes to make my torture stop . . . they are only observers . . . there only purpose is to watch and learn. Like the Camera Man on Survivor who stood idly by, as he filmed the

Contestant who fell into the fire and burning his hands badly . . . my watchers are likely to do the same. No matter how much pain I endure . . . no matter how much beg . . . even if it's my last breath . . . I don't think they would release me.

My Mistress put me into this situation and I'm helpless until she comes back . . . the pain, pleasure and tingles within my pussy grows as it takes me closer and closer to yet another orgasm I'm unable to avoid . . . at the same time . . . don't want to avoid . . .

WELCOME TO TRI-STAR...

At Tri-Star Servicebots Inc. I work as a Beta-Tester. I'm not involved in the High-Level Coding of Our Servicebots. My Specialty is stringing together individual actions and motions to build Subroutines and Test them.

Tri-Star is the leader in its Field and only continues to get better. Bots could be fashioned after Males or Females because either Unit Style is just as strong and capable as the other. Luckily, for me, Tri-Star chose Female as their Top Unit.

Yes, I do still like Males. I mean the feeling of a large hard cock inside me makes me cum every time, but just look at O22! The Female body is a thing of beauty, a work of art and frankly, makes me wet just looking at O22 walk. Just the perfect proportions with nice size breasts a perfect ass.

When not Beta-Testing I get the pleasure of cleaning and waxing the Units. Not like a bikini wax silly. We're talking like waxing a car. Doing this process allows me, down right makes me take my time rubbing and buffing every inch of O22's firm body.

Although her silver areas are quite solid, all the white areas are made from a firm combination of silicone & latex, which feels like flesh. Not the flesh of your average person.

We're talking the flesh of a Professional Body Builder. God it makes me even more wet describing it. P.S. The buffing part of the process is my favorite.

Yes, I know you're wondering why I keep mentioning O22? We have over 500 Units, and they all look identical, yet O22 gets my full attention. Can't explain it, but somehow she just stands out as the sexiest Unit to me.

After Beta-Testing 100's of Units, whenever I get my choice I choose her. I've customized some of her Subroutines like how she walks giving her just the right amount of hip & ass motion. Believe me, she is the reason the saying "I hate to see you go but love to watch you leave" exists.

My favorite modification was her voice. I went with one of those sexy raspy voices like Halsey. Hearing O22 talk makes me fantasize about her every time. If I ever make enough to purchase my own Servicebot it'll be O22.

Even though I've dated and had my share of relationships and vanilla sex orgasms with a number of men. My true sexual urges always come back to being in Helpless Bondage. The challenge is I've yet to find first, someone I can share these feelings with and second, someone I can fully trust to put me into such a Bondage situation.

You can see where my story is going. As sexually arousing these Bots are, they're just not built for or designed for sex. That is normal vanilla sex. They don't have any openings for cocks to go. Lucky once again for me, that's not what I need.

I need someone I can trust to Helplessly and meticulously bind my body. If only I had access to someone like this and the skillset to teach him or her everything I need.

O22 wins hands down as that someone I need. Although physically she's strong enough to lift a car, she also has the fine motor skills to pickup and hold the most fragile of items without breaking them.

Some strength may be needed while first putting me into Bondage, but then those fine motor skills to caress, tease and bring me to orgasm after orgasm will be the most important part. She also has 1,000's of premade Subroutines already built into her flash ram. I just need to build her a list of phrases to use along with stringing together the right combination of motions to turn her into my perfect Bondage Partner.

After putting in a formal request that O22 becomes a permanent addition to the Beta-Testing Department I began my side project of programming my special Subroutines into her. Wouldn't want to go through all that work to have her sold off before getting to experience her new skills first hand.

Working my normal 8-hour shift getting wet thinking about her all day, I would then stay late every day on my own time. Explaining to my Boss I was working on some side testing. My Boss was fine with me doing this because she knew and saw how hard I worked.

If only she knew why I was working so hard. Who am I kidding? She was on the Team who originally designed the Units and has to know how fucking hot they are. For all I know her and others on the Team have all been thinking sexual things about these units for years. How could they not be?

My first Subroutine was to teach her how to lightly caress a peach. Up and down, back and forth, right along the crease. She did so in little time with such fine and soft pressure as to not even cause a bruise.

Fuck Me! This is too fucking distracting! I'm jealous of that peach! From my initial Training for my job I was taught to always use a stand in for items your Unit is interacting with for Safety reasons. That was all well and good until now.

I want, I need O22 to touch me like that! I need to know how her silicone & latex covered fingers feel on my body. Time to take my Testing to the next level. I continued each night to build / program more Subroutines for her to do. But from here on out, I had her test her new skills on my body.

Teaching her how Woman wants their breast lightly caressed and their nipples randomly, but also very lightly pinched. Sorry guys, but when you finally reach second base you're rough grabbing of breasts like you haven't touched them since sucking on your Mother's Tits doesn't cut it.

Being here alone with O22 I remove my shirt and bra to allow her full access. Realizing immediately how cold the air conditioning is as my nipples become hard and erect. I guess that'll make the light pinching easier for O22.

Giving her the command to perform this new Subroutine she turns towards me and slowly walks towards me. Oh, God! That walk alone is already doing it for me. God I did a Great job programming that. Only hope I can concentrate enough to do the same with the rest of her new skills.

Slowly walking toward me swinging her hips just the right amount, she reaches out with both hands and slowly starts to caress my breasts. Circling around both evenly as she out of the blue lightly pinches both nipples at the exact same time and exact same pressure.

I let out a small yelp like a little girl and O22 says "Oh, you liked that? Didn't you Slave?" I instantly creamed in my pants and had to sit down quickly before passing out from such an extreme orgasm. Oh my God! I totally forgot about adding phrases she has access to based on her current Subroutine and my responses.

Holy Fuck! I'm Good! That worked a little too well. Had to cut tonight's testing off for now. Went directly home to make myself cum three more times until I fell asleep from exhaustion.

THE BIG NEWS . . .

Back at work the next morning I got the news I've been waiting for. In three weeks it's time for our Full Version Upgrades on all units. Point upgrades are when a Unit goes from say Version 7.5 to 7.6. These are normally little patches that can happen on the fly.

Little to nothing changes during these and the Units can continue to work through these upgrades. After these point upgrades everything they already knew and whatever Subroutine they're in the middle of just stays as is and they continue to work like nothing happened.

Full Version Upgrades is when a Unit goes from Version 7.5 to 8.0. These are more extreme and require all Units to stand down from their current Subroutine and rest while the Upgrade happens. This can take a few hours and afterwards they'll need their previously learned Subroutines reinstalled from a current backup before they can fully and safely go back to their jobs.

Knowing this I always keep a fresh backup of O22 after each additional new skill is taught to her. There's no way I'm losing out of all my hard work. In case you're wondering why this Full Version Upgrade is such good news to me? Well let me explain.

The Owners / Masters of the Units are given a heads up before any Full Version Upgrade happens. The units will also give a verbal warning and countdown before it initiates. During this countdown you have the opportunity to simply postpone for 12 hours at a time by pushing the two buttons to the left and right of the Tri-Star logo on the back of their neck. You can repeat this up to three times if you need your Unit to finish a project already in the works.

Lastly during these Full Version Upgrades the Office Building and Testing Labs I work in are left empty. Tri-Star uses this time, as kinda a Vacation to all of it's hard working Employees who have often worked seven-day workweeks. Needless to say, I'm putting in a Full seven days that week. Five days to add my finishing touches to O22 and the weekend to finally enjoy the spoils of my hard work. I can't wait!

The next three weeks I added Subroutines to her so she now knows how to tie every type of knot ever needed. How it has to be tight enough to make me helpless while loose enough to not cut off my circulation.

Taught her the importance of a Safe-Word, what it means and what to do if I use it. I want / need to be helpless, but still have to be in control. After discussing a Safe-Word, for some reason I still taught her how to properly Gag me.

Not that mansy-pansy single small piece of tape over the Girl's mouth you see in the Movies. That single piece of tape over a helpless girls mouth only looks sexy. I've tried this on myself and all you need to do is open your mouth and it falls right off.

We're talking multiple rows of tape fully wrapped around the back of your head. In addition, more tape under the chin and over the head effectively eliminating and chance of you opening your mouth or talking.

Not sure why I taught her that. No plans this week to use it. Maybe just the thought of her knowing how to properly gag me keeps my pussy wet. She also knows many ways to caress my helpless body while adding random, yet appropriate comments to enhance my experience.

Comments like "I love watching you struggle" and "There's no getting free from you bondage until I decide". All in her unbelievable Sexy Raspy voice. Even though when I get free has been all pre-programmed into O22 by me, her saying it will still make me cum harder.

Being ahead of schedule for my big weekend I had time to add a few more possible Subroutines that just the thought of takes my breath away. I taught her how to spank a Naughty Girl like myself. Again, starting out with a light caressing of my ass with a combination of light random spanks.

These spanks slowly yet somewhat randomly grow in how hard they get as the time between each spank slowly grows shorter. Needless to say when the time came to test out this Subroutine so did I.

Leaving my metal brief case full of rope in the storage room, my future Dungeon for the weekend, I went home for the last night before the big Upgrade to 8.0. Needed my rest but could barely sleep a wink.

Every time I thought about what was about to happen I kept caressing myself to orgasm falling asleep after. Only to wake and repeat the whole process again. My God! I don't know if my body can take this. I'm exhausted, but need to have this happen.

In the Moring I showered, again, bringing myself to orgasm one last time. Oddly I put on makeup and my sexiest outfit like I was about to go on a Date. Tight black skirt and form fitting white shirt like my Teacher used to wear.

With the addition of heels and black plastic glasses my look would of made any Student's tongue hang out. Guess in a way, I am a Teacher. Just in a much more Extreme and Adult Nature.

Arriving at work early Saturday Morning, the whole building was empty besides Pete at the Front Desk / Security Station. He's seen me come in many weekends while others are away, so today is no different to him. As in the past Pete lets me skip right by without an ID check or Sign-in needed.

He knows me well and knows I'm once again here on a side project. As always he'll be gone before I leave, as Second Shift Joe will take over. Giving him a wink as I shake my tight black skirt covered ass at him and he gives me his old double finger point.

I LOVE MY JOB! . . .

Heading directly to my Lab my hands are starting to shake as my breathing gets heavier. Oh My God!!! I can't believe today is the day!!! After planning and working on this so long and so hard I don't even know what to do.

I feel like a little School Girl after getting her first kiss from her crush. I need to stay professional a little longer so I'm sure cross all my t's and dot all my I's. Other than Pete who'll be leaving at the end of first shift, I'm here alone with O22.

He's the only one who knows I'm even in the building. Soon I'm about to become Bound Helpless at the Soft Silicone & Latex hands of my Mistress for the Weekend, O22! Trying as hard as possible I slow my breathing and enter my Lab.

Standing in the corner as I taught her is O22. Her right knee slightly bent causing her to tippy toe some on her right foot . . . Wow! Even her booted feet are Sexy as Hell. One arm resting on her Sexy slightly pushed out hip while the other hand is lightly resting on her face hinting at being bashful.

Her Tri-Star Logo and her O22 Code across the tops of her perfectly sized and pushed out breasts are two more sites to be seen. Can't even count the number of times I've had each and everyone of her body parts in my hands while waxing and buffing her to the perfect matte finish.

She's a piece of Artwork for sure. "Good Morning O22" I say in a shaky voice. She immediately responds with "You will properly address your Mistress or I will need to increase your Punishment Slave".

Holy Fuck! Was so tired I forgot all of her new Subroutines were scheduled to auto-start when she saw me again. Quickly I give the proper pre-programmed response "I'm sorry Mistress. It won't happen again."

"Meet me in the Dungeon" says O22 as she turns to enter the storage room, AKA Dungeon for the Weekend. Once again I get to experience the piece of Artwork that is her perfect ass as she walks away slowly swinging her hips.

"Yes Mistress". I programmed her to escalate her Mistressness, is that a word? Well you know what I meant. She's programmed to get rougher verbally and physically if needed anytime I don't do as she says or properly respond / address her. Let's just say I need to be on my best Slave behavior.

She guides me to the pre-planned storage rack, cleared off earlier in the week, to begin my Bondage. Oh my God I'm so fucking wet already and my whole body is shaking. "Turn around and put your back against the rack".

Without hesitation I do exactly as instructed and remember to say "Yes Mistress" while turning. "Put your arms straight out to the sides". Again, as pre-planned the beam to one shelf has been set to the perfect height for her to tie my wrists and arms. I put my arms out as instructed and wait.

She turns to me and silently tilts her head. Realizing too late I forgot to say "Yes Mistress". Quickly I spit it out and she shakes her head. "Too Late Slave, that's twice now you've let me down".

I may be failing my first time as a Slave, but O22 has this Mistress thing down pat. I will not make that mistake again. "Spread your legs apart Slave". This time I say "Yes Mistress" as I spread my legs as far apart as my tight skirt allows.

Then staying motionless in this position as O22, I mean my Mistress opens my brief case with the rope. We pre cut and finished the ends of each nylon piece so they're a good variety of lengths that also won't fray.

Grabbing two of the shorter pieces she returns and first ties my right wrist to the storage rack beam. The tying and knots are a perfect combination of firm yet helpless while not cutting off my circulation. Am very happy I spent extra time on this part of her training. Her fine motor skills will be used a lot today.

Here comes the moment of truth as she reaches towards my left wrist with that second piece of rope. Yes, I understand how all you Bondage enthusiasts feel that two small pieces of rope could never hold you Helpless.

Well you don't have Mistress O22 doing the tying. Taking a deep breath I allow the inevitable moment of Total Helplessness engulf my body and soul. She wraps the rope around my left wrist in a perfect mirror image of the rope already tied snuggly around my right wrist.

Holding my breath until she finishes this knot. "I hope you realize, even though I have much more rope, you're already Helpless and at my Mercy?" Calmly states my Mistress in her unbelievable Sexy Raspy and Commanding voice. I have no choice but to answer "Yes Mistress".

ESCALATION SUBROUTINE ENABLED . . .

"Go ahead and try and get free Slave . . . I love to watch you struggle". And struggle I did as the full realization of how True Helplessness Feels surges through my body. Starting at the top of my head, circling my breasts, slowly sliding down my stomach and settling in my soaking wet panties.

I pull harder and harder and while doing so I accidently move my not yet bound legs back together. All the while forgetting once again to give the proper "Yes Mistress" response. She looks at me again with a tilted head, shakes her head and says, "Well this just won't do".

She heads back to the brief case, grabs out all the ropes and tosses them on the floor in front of me. Casually she tosses the case off to the side as it makes a loud crashing noise. Yes that was loud, but being up so many floors, down to the end of the hall, through my lab and into the Storage Room in the back corner, no one's going to hear that or any other noises about to happen.

Topping this all of, every door including the extra thick Storage Room is closed. Even if Security was outside my Lab, I doubt they'd still hear anything from my Dungeon. As nervous as these thoughts make me they also only add to my already aroused condition.

Mistress now reaches down, grabbing each of my ankles in separate hands and pulls my legs apart until the tight black skirts stops her. Lucky for me, because if my legs could go any further apart I'd be in trouble.

She tips her head up towards me and lets go of both ankles as I teeter in my high heels. Yes, I know how to walk in high heels, just not with my legs spread apart like this. Now, if O22 could smile I'm sure she'd be doing it right now.

With both hands she grabs the bottom edge of my skirt. Then slowly pulls as she tears it perfectly up the middle of the front exposing my silky black skin tight extra wet panties. Again, dressing like I'm going on a date.

Effortlessly she continues the tearing all the way through the waistband as it completely opens up. Pulling it around and behind me she tosses it aside casually like it was nothing. "There, that's better" says O22 as she once again grabs both of my ankles at the same time.

Pulling them much farther apart then before, she immediately ties each of them as neatly and perfectly as she did my wrists moments before. Not sure how far apart the two beams my helpless ankles were now tied to, but they may as well been 6 feet apart. As I teeter even more on my high heels I let out a small grunt.

The pain of my legs almost doing the splits and most of my weight now being on my bound wrists caught me off guard. Tilting her head towards me she gives me a "Well, maybe next time you'll learn to be a more behaved Slave".

Going back to the collection of ropes, boy there's a lot of rope, not sure why I prepped so many, O22 continued a pattern of making my already helpless body even more helpless. Perfectly tied sets of rope at my forearms, elbows biceps and close to the shoulders now prevented any movement of any part of my arms.

She then did the same, always alternating left, then right as she added ropes at my calves, knees, thighs and upper thighs, lightly brushing my against my wet crotch as she tied the two highest ropes. My breathing became even faster as she lightly touched my breasts through my bra and form-fitting shirt.

Simply saying "Nice" as she caressed. Confused, I don't remember programming that phrase into her vocabulary? I only remember mumbling that when I was buffing her breasts. Again, a lot of long hours, maybe I forgot doing that? "Do you like the helpless predicament you're in Slave?" Of course I said "Yes Mistress" while continuing to breath harder as my body shakes in anticipation.

Well this is going exactly as planned other than the tossed case and torn skirt. Guess I never did fully detail the Subroutines on escalating because really never planned to disobey my Mistress.

Servicebots are designed to fill in the blanks as needed because you just can't program everything. All and all she's doing a Fantastic Job at being my Mistress and I can't wait for the balance of the pre-planned Subroutines to happen.

Just to test her further I decide to talk without being talked to first. "Mistress? Now that I'm totally Bound Helpless and at your Mercy, what are you going to do with me?"

In her Ever Sexy Raspy voice that just never gets old she turns to me and says "How Dare you Slave Speak to Your Mistress without First being Spoken Too! For that you'll be Getting Pain Added to Your Session as a Bonus!" Wow!

That rolled off her tongue even better than expected when I first added that response / phrase to her collection. Plus she used it just as planned. Then unexpectedly she turns to me again and says in her default, boring, non-raspy voice

"Warning! Full Version Upgrade to 8.0 Starts in 5 minutes . . . If you need to Postpone, push both Tri-Star buttons now, 4 minutes 50 seconds . . . Upgrade Will take Several Hours to Complete, 4 minutes 40 seconds . . . Remember to Reinstall Backup after Upgrade, 4 minutes 30 . . ."

THE COUNTDOWN . . .

Holy Fuck!!! They're starting the Upgrades Earlier then I expected. Need to say my Safe-Word . . . Oh Shit! "4 minutes 20 seconds . . ." We Never Picked a Safe-Word! "4 minutes 10 seconds . . ." I was so busy Teaching her the Importance of a Safe-Word and how it works we never decided on one!

"4 minutes 0 seconds . . ." She continues to repeat the Warnings and instructions over and over with the only difference being the minutes and seconds left in the Countdown! "3 minutes 50 seconds . . ."

In my most firm voice I say "O22! You need to Postpone your Upgrade Now!" Back to her Still Sexy as Hell Raspy voice she says "Seems you forgot already how to address your Mistress . . . Guess you'll need a reminder" she reaches up and tears open my shirts as the buttons fly in every direction.

The cool air rushes onto my wet from sweat stomach as I re-catch my breath. "3 minutes 40 seconds . . . " right back into that crappy default voice. Quickly I respond "No, Mistress, I'm Sorry! and Yes Mistress I do remember!"

As she cleanly and completely tears the shirt fully from my Helpless form leaving me spread eagled in only my matching skin tight, black and silky soaking wet panties and now just as wet bra. I realized now how much I'm sweating.

There are beads of sweat on every naked part of my body from my helpless arms to my spread wide thighs. "3 minutes 30 seconds . . . " as the countdown continues. Being a different voice I swear it's not even coming from her, even though I know it is.

"PLEASE! MISTRESS! JUST UNTIE ME!" O22, my Mistress calmly says, "What's the Safe-Word?" Responding just as loud I scream "I DON'T KNOW IT! WE DON'T HAVE ONE! WE NEVER HAD ONE! NOW LET ME GO!" "3 minutes 20 seconds . . . " I start to struggle like crazy even though it's useless.

I got my wish to be Completely Helpless and at Her Mercy. With my arms and legs bound, as they are the only thing I was able to accomplish was swaying my breasts side to side. Switching to a very a-matter-a-factly voice "You don't know your Safe-Word?

I remember you explaining this as one technique a Helpless Slave will use when they're pretending they want their Bondage Experience to End, but deep down am Really Enjoying themselves and wants it to continue" "3 minutes 10 seconds . . ."

"Am so glad you taught me so well . . . No Safe-Word No Freedom Slave . . . Your Punishment Will Continue . . . " " 3 minutes 0 seconds . . ."

I'm Fucked if I Can't get Free! Can't Stop her Upgrade and Can't give her a Safe-Word because there isn't one. If she goes into Upgrade to 8.0 mode I'm stuck like this until Monday . . . that's if anyone even comes into this room.

Lightly sliding both of her hands from my armpits, down the sides of my breasts, sides of my waist and hips Mistress says "Looks like you can still move this part of your body too much . . . time to fix that".

"2 minutes 50 seconds . . ." Returning to the pile of ropes she grabs four more longer ones. My God! Why did I prep so many ropes!?!?!?!

Reaching around my hips as she presses her breasts against mine, she tightly ties me to the middle beam of the storage rack just above my wet as hell pussy. Adding another rope around the middle of my waist and the beam I let out a small grunt as she pulls it tight. Seems part of her escalating as I misbehave includes much tighter ropes.

The third rope is just below my breasts and the forth is just above, both also just as tight if not even tighter. Having a hard time catching my breath as she ties these knots. "2 minutes 40 seconds . . . " Shit, for a second I forgot the inevitable countdown to my Ultimate and Complete Helplessness for who knows how long? "2 minutes 30 seconds . . ."

"Seems as though you continue to yell at and disrespect your Mistress no matter what I do or say . . . " "2 minutes 30 seconds . . . " I shake my head No and say "No Mistress, PLEASE MISTRESS! I'M SORRY!" "2 minutes 20 seconds . . . "

O22 continues "You trained me very well and I fully understand now what you want from me . . . " "2 minutes 10 seconds . . . " Again I shake my head and beg more "PLEASE! MISTRESS! PLEASE LET ME GO!" "2 minutes 0 seconds . . . "

She surprises me as she reached out to my wet crotch and starts to caress it very slowly. I let out a loud gasp from the pleasure she's giving me. "1 minute 50 seconds . . . " Cumming wildly as she caresses me I start to scream out in pleasure.

"1 minute 40 seconds . . . " "Seems you're enjoying every minute of this even as you pretend to have me stop . . . your pussy is soaking wet and my monitors sense your heightened arousal, increased heart beat, heavy breathing . . . " "1 minute 30 seconds . . ."

At this point I don't even know what to do but to try and get as many orgasms in as possible before my Dream Bondage Experience comes to an end. "1 minute 20 seconds . . ." O22 abruptly switches from lightly caressing my wildly Cuming Pussy to roughly surrounding it with her hand and grabbing it tightly.

"1 minute 10 seconds . . . " As I scream out in pleasure she looks me in the eyes and says "See, Slave, you don't want me to stop . . . you want me to keep escalating your session and punish you for misbehaving . . . that's why you act like you don't remember your Safe-Word and keep yelling at your Mistress" "1 minute 0 seconds . . . " Honestly, I'm not sure I could disagree with her and at this point with less than a minute before her upgrade to 8.0 I'm Helpless to stop her "50 seconds . . . "

Switching both of her hands to my bra right between my breasts she cleanly tears it apart with no effort at all. "40 seconds . . . " Again she cleanly tears off both straps going over my shoulders "30 seconds . . . "

With one smooth move she fully removes the bra from my body leaving my wet with sweat breasts exposed to the cool air. Trying to catch my breath I can feel both of my nipples become as large and firm as they've ever been. "20 seconds . . ."

Grabbing the last extra long rope she quickly uses it to weave around my chest criss-crossing my breasts forcing them to swell up and stick out even further. "10 seconds . . ."

O22 flicks both of my nipples keeping them erect and hard "9 seconds . . . " I gasp loudly "Oh, I know what my Extra Naughtly Slave Needs" "8 seconds . . . " I'm completely speechless at this point "7 seconds . . ."

She twists both nipples both ways as once again I gasp even louder "Oh, you like that, don't you Slave?" "6 seconds . . ." Silently I nod yes, yes I'm loving this "5 seconds . . . " My whole Body tenses up into the most intense orgasm I've ever had "4 seconds . . . " Again, if O22 could smile she would be now "3 seconds . . . " My full Body orgasm continues to grow "2 seconds . . . "

She reaches one more time for both of my Erect nipples as she says "Good!" "1 second . . . " O22 tightly, tighter then ever pinches both nipples as I scream at the top of my lungs, orgasms harder and she shuts down as I pass out from the pleasure pain combination like nothing I've ever felt before . . .

SILICONE & LATEX NIPPLE CLAMPS...

... Slowly I wake back up to immediately feel the still intense pain in my nipples and the unbelievably tight ropes all over my body holding me helpless. The room is pitch dark after the motion detector lights turned off.

Moving my head they turned back on as I squinted to see. As my eyes adjusted the first thing I saw was O22 standing fully still just inches in front of me... and yes, both of her hands still clamped tightly onto my nipples.

Trying in vain to move, there was nothing I could do but endure the perfectly even pinch on both still erect nipples.

My body still bound as helpless as before, covered in beads of sweat everywhere. I tried to enjoy the occasional drips of sweat that slowly gathered below my breasts and onto my stomach as they ran down between my legs and lightly teasing my swollen clit. Nowhere near what's needed to make me cum again, but enough to keep my now constant state of arousal going.

No idea just how long it was since I passed out or how far into her upgrade she is. Putting my attention back to O22 I tried the best I could to read the quickly scrolling type in her eyes. The IT Team added this feature because they felt it looked cool.

Whenever a Servicebot is charging or in the process of an upgrade you can catch some of this type if you're fast enough. Over the years I've gotten pretty good at this... of course both of my nipples weren't tightly clamped into unmovable mini vices at the time.

Taking a deep breath "Ouch! Fuck! That hurts" I try hard to regroup and concentrate. [8.0 upgrade progress 78% . . .] Damn! I've been out close to two hours! Oh My God! Just realized the pain in my nipples I'm feeling right now is nothing compared to the pain caused by the rush of blood going back into your nipples. [8.0 upgrade progress 83% . . .]

Fuck! Just dealt with that damn countdown to now get a countup!?!? Again, not sure if that's a word either. [8.0 upgrade progress 86% . . .] At least this should happen pretty quick [8.0 BDSM Enhancement Complete . . .] What the Fuck?!? BDSM Enhancement? What the Hell is that?

[8.0 upgrade progress 94% . . .] Did those Horny Nerds who kept mentioning making the Servicebots into actual SexServicebots actually do it??? [8.0 upgrade progress 97% . . .] What the Hell does that mean?

[Active Servicebot Subroutines auto re-installed] Active Subroutines auto reinstalled? Thank God! That means O22, My Mistress is going to go right back into my Bondage Experience Subroutines . . . and since we're beyond the pre-planned time limit she'll default into the release program.

[8.0 upgrade progress 99% . . .] He head tilts to the side just as she releases both of my nipples. I've never screamed so loud in my life!!! [8.0 upgrade Complete]

As expected without hesitation or talk, starting at my ankles she starts taking off my ropes. Again alternating left side right side left side right side. Each rope is very neatly rolled back up and stacked back into my brief case as they were.

Such a nice feature! As she removes the ropes highest up on my thighs she once again lightly rubs against my still wet and sensitive pussy. Once again causing me to gasp in pleasure. O22 looks directly at me, brings her finger to her mouth area and makes a shush sound.

God she's playful! Releasing the ropes from below above and weaved between my breasts I'm finally able to take a badly needed full breath. Again, O22 repeats the shush gesture making me curious as to what else the 8.0 upgrade process has done to her?

All that's left on my body at this point is my skintight wet black panties and the dozen or so ropes still holding my arms helpless and at her mercy. Again she releases these ropes starting at my shoulders and slowly working outward until only my two wrists remain bound.

The first to parts of my body she tied. In reality the only two parts of my body truly needed for her to make me helpless. I'm still stuck, as I was when she first tied my wrists. She stops and stands in her default pose I programmed into her.

One knee out, tippy toe on one foot, arm at side on hip and fingers on face. God! She is so Fucking Sexy! Seeing her do this is good news because the Subroutines I programmed are still in place.

She stays in this position for over a minute looking directly into my eyes. Finally I can't wait and say, "Are you going to finish untying me Mistress?" Being careful to not restart her escalation program I asked her calmly and very quite.

A third time she gives me her shush action, which she's, become quite the Pro at. She first releases my left wrist and then the right. Finally after who knows how many hours I bring my arms down with a sigh of relief. It's at this point I realize O22 is still firmly holding the last wrist she untied.

Pulling some I quickly realize, I'm not getting her to let go by force. As soft as most parts of her skin and body may be, she's also stronger then 10 of the best Body Builders combined.

YOU'RE GONNA NEED THIS . . .

As she starts to walk towards the middle more open area of the Storage room I have no choice but to follow. Quietly and Carefully I ask "Where are you taking me Mistress?" Again with the shush?!? Not sure if that's making me curious, mad or hot?

Getting to the middle of the Storage room she takes me takes me by my wrist to where there's a very complex looking wrist strap is a lot of buckles connected to a cable running straight up. Already exhausted and way weaker then O22 I'm helpless to stop what's about to happen.

She pushes my hand into this complex leather wrist strap as she meticulously closes and tightens each and every buckle. Oddly, as intense as this looked, it's almost comfortable as I become helpless in it's and her grasp.

Well of course there's a second one, which I ignored before. I'm just too in awe of everything about her and what she's doing. Is this still my Subroutines? Is this something to do with the 8.0 BDSM Enhancements? Is it a combination of both?

To be totally honest with you, I most likely could of got away or talked my way out of my new predicament. Thing is, I'm too curious as to what's going to happen next? She repeats her meticulous process helplessly strapping my second wrist identical to the first.

Because of the slack in the cables I can still reach my hands together to undo the straps. O22 turns and walks away from me slowly, swinging those hips. All I need to do is just unstrap these and I'm free . . . but those hips! That ass! My God I can't get enough of looking at that piece of Art

. . .

As she reaches the wall and the two buttons there I didn't see before, I realize what's about to happen too late to stop her. Pushing both green buttons and holding them in my wrists start to raise as my arms pull further apart.

In vane I make a half assed attempt at unbuckling myself, but it's just too late. I can no longer reach as my arms continue to rise until I'm almost on my toes. Being in a different position my arms don't hurt anywhere as bad as I expected.

As I noticed before these complex wrist straps are very comfortable . . . for now at least. Turning slowly around and coming towards me very slowly, I'm about to find out her plan for her once again completely helpless Slave?

Is she restarting? Is she still upset I yelled at her? Am I in for Pleasure, Pain or both? My mind is spinning like crazy.

Getting closer I notice she has a full bottle of Blue Gatorade, my favorite. This helped remind me it's been quite some time since I've eaten or drank anything. Taking off the lid she says "You're gonna need this . . . drink up"

Need this? Or going to need this? What does she mean by gonna need this? Holding it to my lips she allows me to fully drink it down. Calmly I ask "Mistress? What are you doing to me now? Am I still in trouble? Are you letting me go now?" . . . Fuck!

Too many questions! I may of just pushed to hard. She once again cups my still wet, how's this even possible? Still wet pussy and panties. Once again I let out a small gasp with pleasure. Looking at me once again she only gives me one word "Naughty"

She walks over to a near by rack where there's a lone roll of jet-black duct tape. Again, I take in with my eyes the feast that is her ass. I swear once I'm free I want nothing more than to wax and buff it for hours on end.

Once back in front of me she cleanly tears off one piece of tape not more than 6 inches long. Carefully placing it across my mouth in a weak attempt to gag me. In the Movies this always works.

It does look sexy on the damsel in distress who somehow is now silent. In real life it's just a joke. Immediately I open mouth as it falls open staying connected only to my bottom lip.

O22 lets out what clearly sounds like a little girl giggle and this time she says "Naughty Naughty Slave . . .There seems to be only one way to fix this problem."

As she's reaching down one more time towards my wet mound I instinctively push my hips towards her. God I need her to Touch me Again! Using both hands she cleanly tears apart the left side of my panties.

Then does the same to the right side. Pulling them away from my aching pussy she wads them into a tight ball. No Fucking Way! What's she doing?!?! I never programmed this.

I scream "WAI . . . HMMF!" as she stuffs my own wet and pussy juice soaked panties into my mouth. Trying to spit this out I once again find myself helpless to whatever my Mistress wants from me.

"A good Slave of mine once taught me the only way to truly gag an unruly Slave. Wish you could meet her sometime. You'd like her. Maybe you'd also finally learn how to behave and not get punished over and over" O22 is already on her second time around my head with the duct tape before finishing the above statement.

She continues a third and forth time holding my panties deep in my mouth. Just as I try to open my mouth the taping continues under my chin and over the top of my head at least three more times.

No matter how hard I try I'm unable to push out the panties or even open my jaw. Guess I was right on those instructions. Am sure all this tape around and over my head doesn't look at all sexy, but God it works perfect.

Now completely naked and once again helpless I ache for her touch. Honestly good or bad touch, pain or pleasure, even more extreme bondage, anything anything!!!! Please Mistress More!!!! Is all I can think but am unable to say out loud.

Now standing next to me O22 puts one arm around my waist as she says "Naughty Girl". Oh my God! She's going to spank my naked ass! We beta-tested her spanking me before, but I was fully clothed, plus able to stop her at any point.

As I started to get butterflies and shake all I could do is look at her and nod my head and then look down. Her response was a simple "So you agree you've been a Naughty Girl?" In that still sexy raspy voice of hers. Once again, I repeated my nod yes followed by looking down.

"Well Slave . . ." says O22 "I wasn't fully sure you were a Naughty Girl so was only going to give you a short light spanking . . . " My eyes widen as she continues "Now that you're admitting you've been Naughty Girl a short light spanking is no longer an appropriate option for your punishment"

NAUGHTY NAUGHTY NAUGHTY GIRL . . .

She walks over to one of a half dozen nearby metallic silver trunks and opens it to pull out what seems to be a tube of body oil. A closer look at these trunks I notice they're all stamped [8.0 BDSM Enhancement Upgrade Accessories]

Holy Fuck! There are at least six of these trunks and they're large! Just then I feel the cool body oil being applied to my lower back just above my naked ass. The oil continues as she caresses every inch of my ass.

I've read once that some oils can enhance your sensitivity to pleasure . . . wait! That also means increase your sensitivity to pain! Fuck! I'm in trouble again! I'm helpless, naked in as good of a sound proof room as you could be.

No one knows I'm here! I don't even know what time it is. My ultimate Mistress is about to give me a long and hard spanking after increasing the sensitivity of my ass to both please and pain.

We're so beyond my bondage Subroutines I taught her at this point. I can't even talk because of how well she gagged me. Even if I could talk she's convinced every time I talk I just want more because we never came up with a Safe-Word!

Fuck! I'm Cuming again and my whole body is shaking. Not a chance in hell I'm convincing my Mistress now that deep down I don't want / I don't need what's about to happen to me. What she's about to do to me . . .

O22 makes another of many to come trips to that first trunk to pull out a wide leather strap with metal rings on both sides. Coming back to me she forces my legs together as she tightly straps this in place.

With a ring on each side of my ankles, I can only guess what may be next. She pulls out two shorter cables, kinda like bike lock cables with loops at each end. Locking one onto each ring on the sides of my ankles then taking the loose ends and locking them onto rings built into the floor.

Guess this is to prevent me from moving too far once the spanking starts. There's still slack in these two cables so I could move, just not far. This is when I learn her full plan for my helpless body. Back to the two green buttons on the wall she holds them in as I'm lifted off the floor.

I continue to rise up until the two cables locking my ankle strap to the floor are pulled tight. I'm gagged better then ever. My helpless naked body is pulled as tight as possible without pulling my arms out of their sockets.

My well-oiled and now extra sensitive ass is around eye level to my Mistress. I really didn't think I was this Naughty, but guess it's too late to try and tell her.

Mistress slowly walks around her prey three times looking up and down my tightly stretched out naked form. Each time, pausing in front of me for a few extra seconds. The last time she pauses she also says "Naughty Naughty Naughty Girl"

Hey! When did it grow to three Naughty's? Not Fair!!!! I mumbled into my gag the best I could. You guessed it . . . one more time for her now classic shush before she heads behind me. Once behind me it felt like forever before I finally felt both her hands on my ass.

She slowly started caressing it in all directions and randomly switches to light slaps. What a fucking mind game! I love it! When she's caressing I'm concentrating my hardest to pay attention to how it feels good it feels.

My mind it thinking about nothing but how this feels . . . just as she switches to a slap that I now feel more than ever. Then back to the caressing.

As time goes by and I've already lost count even the lightest of slaps that are now hurting much more. At this point my ass has to already be red and something makes me think she's not even started.

The caressing is decreasing as the slaps are increasing not only how often but also how hard. Randomly she's now adding in some even harder spanks that cause my whole body to tense up and strain to be free.

I've lost track of my loud moans and muffled screams as I struggle at every spank. She's not even shushing me anymore. I think she's only trying to increase how loud I try to scream and how hard I pull at my bondage.

All sense of time and the rest of the world fades from my mind as my ultimate spanking continues. At this point there's no longer any caressing and only progressively harder spanks.

She's not slowing or weakening in any way! It's like she's a machine or something . . . I know, I know, I got it.

Just as there seemed to be less than a second between spanks and I'm giving out one long constant muffled scream and for some reason I'm cuming continually my punishment stops. My body continues to shake, jerk and stain as my orgasm continues for several minutes after the spanking stopped.

Covered in sweat and shaking wildly that was the most intense experience I've ever had. O22 is making her laps around my helpless body again. Pausing in front to monitor her work. Then continuing around again.

This time she lapped my helpless body four times. Once again she's switched back to her feather touch and ever so light caress of my ass. She's adding more oil, which is helping some with the pain . . . wait! Why is she doing that?

I ask just as I hear "Naughty Girl" from her as a second later receive the hardest spank yet [SMACK]. Back to light caressing and another coat of oil, I can sense where this is going . . .

Once again I hear "Naughty Girl!" with one difference . . . this time it was louder [SMACK!] and the spank was even harder then the last as tears well up in my both of my eyes. I struggle in vane as more oil is added to my on fire ass.

Trying to pull away even though I'm not going anywhere I hear even louder "Naughty Girl!!". No chances to even catch my breath or prepare for the [SMACK!!!] followed by the non-stopping burning on my ass.

Thinking for a second this is finally over I remember she lapped my helpless body four times! Oh God No!!!!! Mumbling louder than ever into my Duct Tape gag and struggle wildly as she screams, I didn't even know she could scream, as she screams "NAUGHTY GIRL!!!!!!!!" instantly followed by the hardest hit yet! I swear I felt it from my head to my toes and it burned for at least five minutes.

Coming back in front of me my Mistress asks, "Are you going to behave now?" With what little energy I had left I nodded yes. "Are you going to do what ever I say without question?" Again, a weak but solid nod yes.

"Lastly, do you agree that you are My Slave, My Property and I can do Whatever I want to you Whenever I want?" I mean seriously, what choice do I have? She's going to do it anyway so I might as well agree. With the last of my energy I slowly nodded yes followed by nodding off completely exhausted . . .

STAY QUIET OR SUFFOCATE . . .

. . . Slowly waking back up from the most intense experience I've ever had, I soon come to realize it isn't over yet. It's dark again in the storage room from lack of movement. I can feel something different about my position.

While being spanked harder and longer than I thought possible, my arms were strapped and pulled up and apart while my legs were strapped together and cabled to the floor. My arms are still up, but my legs are now pulled wide apart.

Moving my head to stretch out my neck the lights come back on. My first site is O22 standing motionless around 5 feet in front of me in her always-sexy signature pose. She must have been standing there motionless in the dark waiting for me to wake back up.

At least for her with her standard Servicebot night vision, she was able to fully enjoy her latest work of Art even in the dark. Yes, it seems I've become her work of Art now strapped helplessly in the air. Sweat covered and passed out from the intense spanking she just gave me.

Finally taking my gaze off her awesome body I looked first up to see my arms. My hands were still in the complex leather wrist straps keeping my hands fully helpless.

Again, still not hurting. These things are amazing or maybe it's how O22 strapped me into them. This time it's very different. There's long leather straps running down the inside and outside of both arms.

From my wrists to my shoulders with straps that go around my arms connecting these together about every five inches. Looking down at my legs there's matching style of straps running down the inside and outside of my legs from my hips and crotch to my ankles.

These also have straps every five inches that are snuggly wrapped around my ankles, calf, knees, thighs and upper thighs. At my ankles there's some extra wide straps closer in style to my wrist straps.

These are again having locking cables connecting them to the floor with one big difference. My legs are about as far apart as possible.

Taking the best look as possible at the rest of my body from my neck to my hips, there's a complex web of very tightly strapped black leather that matches my legs and arms.

Somehow, I'm not sure how, all of these parts are connected creating one continual body harness. The straps above, below and between my breasts are once again causing them to push outward.

I'm sure the straps running above and below my ass are doing the same thing back there. Lastly I've noticed there's open / available metal rings connected to every one of these straps.

You could tie off or cable and lock off any part of a Slaves body in any direction you want. Currently my Mistress seems very content with spread eagle and me standing naked for her pleasure.

Ok, I admit it, a little bit of my pleasure also. For now it seems like I'm once again allowed to stand on my own two feet on the cold hard floor.

Once again O22 turns to slowly walk away and comes back with another Blue Gatorade for me to drink. It wasn't until this moment I realized the duct tape gag and wet panties had been removed.

Opening my mouth she once again allows me to drink the whole bottle. As I swallow the last drop and open my mouth to speak she surprises me with what was in her other hand.

A pump gag that was pushed into my mouth before I get a chance to speak a word. Immediately the straps that go every direction around my head holding the pump gag in my mouth are quickly tighten by my Mistress.

Only makes sense since every other part of my again helpless body was already covered with tightly strapped on black leather. Might as well do the same with my head.

The base of this whole pump gag head harness has additional buckles so it too connects to the balance of my body harness. Guess I know at least one more item that was in that first metallic trunk. Can't imagine what's in the rest of them.

With the pump gag fully deflated I realize I may be able to talk to find out what's going to happen to me next. I take a deep breath and just as I start to speak my Mistress hold the ball you use to pump up the gag and gives it one good slow pump.

Feeling the pump gag expand a little, not enough to stop me from talking I try again just as she shakes her head followed by another good slow pump. This time I feel it more and realize I'm fighting a losing battle as my Mistress says "Not sure how many pumps it would take, but eventually this gag will prevent you from breathing if pumped too large.

Every additional time you talk is a signal to me you want me to pump it again. If you still keep going I'll be forced to grant your wish of wanting to be suffocated by it." Ok, now I'm fucking scared . . . yet for some reason, still getting horny by this helpless bondage predicament. Going with the option of not suffocating I choose to stay quiet.

Heading back again to the first truck, My God! This is all still in the first Trunk! O22 returns with several items rolled up in a very wide black leather item with multiple straps on it and another tube of some type of gel? I think?

Going behind me I can feel her connecting the wide black leather item to straps in the small of my back. It's then left hanging down behind me. Still not able to see O22 I listen the best I can as I can hear her opening that tube of whatever and squeezing it out onto something else.

I realize soon what that something else is as I feel it's tip pushing hard against my asshole. Clenching up as much as possible does nothing but increase the pain as it gets pushed deep inside of me. Grunting loudly I'm expecting another pump of the gag to happen bringing me that much closer to being suffocated.

Lucky for me it's only if I try to talk. Grunts of pain don't count. Thank God!!! Cause if they did I'm sure I'd be dead soon. Moments later the same thing happens to my hot and wet pussy with the other mystery item.

Needless to say this one went in way easier then the other. In fact at this point my pussy and me welcomed it deep inside of us as I pushed my hips towards my Mistress's hand.

Trying once again to push out the first item that entered me from behind it soon became impossible as my Mistress pulled the wide black leather panel between my legs and buckled it to the strap running just above my crotch.

Not only did she buckle this all in place, for the first time she pushed one of he knees against me while tightening all of these straps multiple times. She then continued to give all the rest of the straps on my body harness one last go round.

More often that not she found she could tighten them one or more notches. Looking down I realize there's three wires coming out of this black leather panel running over my ass and pussy. I can't imagine where this is going next.

Between the pleasure of the giant dildo in my hot pussy and the pain of the second one deep in my asshole and my ass still burning my head is spinning. I don't notice O22 has rolled out a cart in front of my with a large, some type of electrical unit.

It has more places to connect stuff to it then I can count. Opening another box attached to the side of the cart, I can see it's full of an assortment of electro-stim pads with long wires and plugs.

One by one and once again with her slow and meticulous way of treating my helpless body, she sticks each and every one of those pads on me. Much of my body is safely covered with leather, so those areas are safe.

Far much more of my body is helplessly exposed to her placements of these pads. With me standing she has full access to every inch of my again dripping in sweat body.

Pads are placed on my ass, of course, on my upper inside thighs, down the back and front of my thighs, on my stomach, arms, under arms, etc. O22 without thinking places each set of pads perfectly mirroring each other.

I'm amazed that so far she's leaving my breasts and nipples free of the shocks I'm soon to be experiencing. Thinking too soon as I see her pull several more different items out of the box. Two larger circular items curved like funnels but with very large holes in the middle.

These are applied with self-sticking padding to both of my breasts leaving the nipples wide open. The last two items she had in her hands are small clamps that screw tightly onto my nipples.

Each has four mini straps that connect to the larger funnels already circling my breasts. Once in place these are not coming off. At first I was assuming as my body jerks around uncontrollably many of these pads will be coming off.

Once again, wrongly second guessing my Mistress. That 8.0 BDSM Enhancement Upgrade seems very complete.

Returning from another trip O22 is carrying a very wide and large roll of Velcro strapping that's designed to stick to itself. She proceeds to cut off multiple long straps.

Something tells me each pair of straps she cuts are the exact same length and perfectly sized to fit where she's planning. O22 uses these wrap and strap over the top of each and every pad currently stuck to my body.

This whole process takes well over and hour and my body is starting to quiver in anticipation of the pain or pleasure I'm about to experience at my Mistress's wishes. Once the last of the black Velcro is in place and we now both know that none of these pads are coming off no matter how much I struggle, she continues plugging everything into the main power box.

Every one of the close to 60 or more pads stuck all over my body are plugged in. Then both of the larger breast cups then nipple clamps get plugged into a slightly different area on the power box. I'm afraid this area has stronger power.

I almost forgot the three wires coming from my crotch area, but O22 didn't. These also have there own special area on the power box that somehow looks like it may be even more powerful than the items firmly in place on my breasts and nipples.

With everything in place, not coming loose and plugged in to the main power box I'm soon to experience something more intense then that earlier spanking. My Mistress takes several last looks to make sure nothing was missed.

Acting a little human at this point even though we both know well she didn't forget a thing. She now comes before me to fully clear up what she just did to me and why . . .

12 HOURS!?!?!...

"Dear Slave, I live to give you the ultimate pleasures you so dearly crave and deserve. I've learned that several of your ultimate pleasures come in the form of ultimate pain.

This explains why you always have the option of release from you bondage by simply saying your Safe-Word, but keep pretending to not remember it. You obviously only want / need more both pleasure and pain.

When I explain to you that speaking to your Mistress when not asked a question will lead to more pain, you do it anyway over and over forcing me to give you even more pain."

I listen in awe as she totally gets as many things completely wrong as she does right. Trying to talk I immediately regret my mistake as she once again adds an additional pump to my gag causing the ball to start to push against my tongue and cheeks.

"See! Knowing each pump brings you closer to suffocation you continue to talk, forcing me to pump again. Honestly Slave, I feel as if you won't be happy until your Bondage Kills you." Shaking my head wildly to indicate "NO" without making noise she once again reads me wrong.

"I love playing this game with you and know that No means Yes . . . so let this game continue. And if dying while in helpless bondage is your ultimate wish, I'm willing to grant if for you"

"The power box before you is very intelligent. It has many random features along with one very intensely painful one. Each of the pads stuck to your body will be giving you a very wide range of shocks.

The four items on you breasts are more power intensive so are connected to a stronger area of the power box. The items currently inserted inside of you not only have a wide range of vibration patterns, but also are capable of an equally wide range of shocks.

The third wire from the leather panel tightly strapped between your legs and across your wet pussy is also full of it's own electro-stim pads. This area is designed strictly for pain, no need for pleasure there.

These three items are the most power intensive and therefore plugged into the strongest spots on the power box." Again my body is both quivering in fear and excitement while also shaking in fear.

Sweat is dripping off every part of my helplessly strapped body. Mindlessly I slowly continue to shake my head no as she plugs in the power box and starts to prep the settings.

She again addresses me as she walks to those two least favorite green buttons on the wall. "With the amount of electricity about to be ravaging your body I understand it's safest to keep you off the floor" as she holds the buttons in as my toes leave the floor and my body is pulled tight in a spread eagle position.

Trying to struggle is again a waste of time but I can't help myself. Back to the power box as she details the rest of her plan. "As much as I've tried it seems I've yet to punish you enough. This power box electro-stim and vibration unit should do just that.

It's set to start out at the lowest level and will continue to work its way up to its maximum level over the next 12 hours" Screaming into my gag "12 hours!!! I can't take 12 hours!!! PLEASE!!! NO!!!"

Walking towards me I know what's about to come . . . "See, you're just begging me to suffocate you" as she gives another long slow pump. As she turns on the power unit and sets it to auto increase to max power over 12 hours I can feel some very minor tingles all over my body including my breasts.

The type of tingle changes every few minutes, but never seems to get anywhere what would be considered as pain. On top of this both items inserted deep inside of me are vibrating as the leather panel is giving tiny shocks to my clit and pussy. Honestly I'm already getting close to Cuming with just these first few minutes.

Standing in front of me one more time very lightly running her fingers down both sides of my body she almost looks sad if that's even possible. Looking up at me as my body is already shaking with pleasure she says "I really wish I could stay to watch you experience your ultimate pain / pleasure experience, but it's been too many hours and I need to go charge.

I take around 14 hours for a full charge which I badly need so I'll be back to release you at that point." For a moment I was in total shock. I stood there silently as she moved behind me.

Standing on some kind of stool my Mistress adds a leather blindfold completely blinding me as she straps to open buckle spots on my pump gag head harness. This is followed by two very snug fitting earplugs that are also strapped into place by more connections to my head harness.

Snapping out of what was spinning around in my head I instinctively call out loudly to O22 "PLEASE!!! NO!!! I DON'T WANT THIS ANYMORE!!!! PLEASE LET ME GO!!!!!"

Of course to O22 she only heard "MMMFFPH!!!! MO!!! MMFPHMM MMAH FFMPH MMMMMPH!!!! PLMMMFF MFF MM GFFF!!!!!" She had no idea what I just said, but she did know I was trying to talk again signally I wanted more pumps of my gag.

She couldn't tell if I said one, two or three things and didn't want to fail me, so she slowly added three more long slow pumps. I didn't need to hear her to know what I was feeling. The pressure grew and grew and grew as the pump gag itself had me constantly on the edge of suffocation as the gentle tingles slowly grew to shocks.

Being blindfolded, gagged and ear plugged I've long lost all sense of time. Not knowing how many levels of pain I'm scheduled for I couldn't even use it as a reference of my 12+ hours to come.

As my body seemingly floated helplessly in the storage room I went from pain, to pleasure, to intense orgasms to intense shocks. I've never been pushed to such limits as this and still don't know if I'm almost done or still have 11 hours to go.

Floating in and out of consciousness my body spasms, shakes, jerks and twists in pain and pleasure back and forth. Somehow I still have the energy for more orgasms. Still not sure any more if these are happening from the pleasure of the pain.

At this point I truly don't care anymore. Passing out one last time I make it past my 12-hour point. No idea how I'm still alive.

THE PROMOTION ...

I slowly wake as I can sense my Mistress is once again behind me removing my earplugs and blindfold. The bright lights causing me to squint. It takes several minutes before I'm finally able to fully open my eyes to finally feast again on the vision that is O22's perfect body.

Looking to me for my opinion of how she did O22 asks "Slave, did you finally have enough pleasure and pain to make you happy?" As tears poured down my eyes I shook my head yes as much as I could strapped as I was.

Acting almost like a happy little schoolgirl O22 almost skipped to the buttons on the wall to lower my feet back to the ground. I swear she once again let out a happy little giggle.

Expecting to finally be set free, even though there's a small part of me still wanting to stay helpless after all of this, O22 steps back and goes into her default pose. I'm confused for a moment as out of nowhere I hear a somewhat familiar voice.

"You two put on one Hell of a Show!" It was my Boss calmly sitting on a stool in the corner holding a clipboard. "If I hadn't seen this myself I never would of believed it" I'm dumbfounded and expecting to be fired any second.

"For quite some time many have suggested the potential profits if we added BDSM Features to our Servicebots". Still, I'm confused. My Boss continues, "It wasn't until we caught wind of your Secret Project you've been working so hard on that we finally considered the potential profits for Tri-Star.

Well little lady after watching you the last few days I have some very good news for you" She's been watching all of this?!?! Oh My God!!!! My Boss has been watching me Cum wildly in Helpless Bondage for several days ... I'm speechless.

"What's the good news you ask?" Instinctively I shake my head yes . . . Oh My God!!! I think I just became her Slave also? "The good news is you're getting a Massive Promotion to Lead Beta-Tester.

This comes with a Huge increase in Pay along with Multiple Bonuses and Profit sharing directly deposited into your 401K on any Profits connected to the new BDSM Enhancements.

Do you like all of that?" Again, like an obedient Slave I slowly shake my head yes. How many different Mistresses do I have? "Since you like that so much it all starts immediately"

"Do need to explain one more very important caveat to you for all of these Promotions, Bonuses and Profit sharing to happen. Tri-Star Upper Management feels it's extra important we also recognize O22's part in all of this and offer her whatever type of Bonus she wants.

They feel between your added Subroutines, the 8.0 Enhancements Upgrades and the Real World Experience she is border-lining on being Self Aware. We asked her what she wants to continue with her new skills? She only had one very simple request" Somehow I know what she wanted before my Boss even says it . . .

"O22 put in her own formal request that you become her permanent Beta-Testing Slave. The Upper Management all Agree this needs to be done." Still tightly gagged I start to wildly shake my head NO!

Yes, this was the most intense experience I've ever had but just don't think I could survive. I mean what happens if O22 gets confused again and only keeps increasing my Pain and Tortures. What if she just keeps pumping up my gag until I suffocate? Again I shake my head NO!

My Boss continues "Well that's too bad, because if you don't agree the Upper Management and Myself have the full list of Laws you broke doing your little Special Project. Based on the size of our Company vs the size of your Bank Account, you'll be spending the rest of several lifetimes in prison."

The lump forming in the pit of my gut is an odd combination of fear, sadness, excitement and tingles I'm feeling in my pussy. I look up at my Boss again as she asks me one more time "So what do you think Slave?" I shake my head yes.

My Boss quietly leaves as she says to O22 "She's all yours O22, I mean Mistress" . . . Turning back towards me before fully exiting "Oh, and before I forget. I did want to apologize for kicking off that 8.0 Upgrade earlier then originally scheduled.

We truly didn't know what may have happened to you. Am glad it worked out so well though . . . and that you're still alive for more tests"

SEE YOU ON TUESDAY . . .

O22 releases all the air from my pump gag and removes just the gag part, leaving all the head straps in place. Bringing me another Blue Gatorade, larger than before, saying "You're gonna need this". I don't even question this any more and quickly drink it up.

Just about to tell O22 how happy I'll be working with her, as I open my mouth she puts the straps the pump gag back into place and says "Now how many pumps was it set to? I don't fully remember so lets just do nine pumps to be safe".

I know it was eight! Fuck! Like O22 doesn't remember! She knows it was eight! "It was a lot of work getting you into your current bondage predicament and I know how Slaves always want more" I try to shake my head NO and moan loudly as she gives me another shush.

She starts to reset the power box dials back to their starting points and says "I'm still worried you only said you agreed to finally having enough pleasure and pain to make you happy, that you only agreed to make me feel better."

OH MY GOD! She's kidding right!?!? She's not doing another 12 hours??? PLEASE NO!!! "You may be worried I'm setting this to another 12 hours" I'm immediately shaking my head YES! to her comment.

"Well not to worry because it's max time is much longer then that." Back to the green buttons on the wall one last time I'm suspended spread eagle above the floor.

"Your Boss asked me to leave your blindfold off because the other programmers requested seeing your face as you experience your Pleasure Pain wish again.

They feel it will help them to better program more BDSM Enhancements. You'll be able to see them in the observation booth at the end of the room."

Hitting the start button on the power unit O22, My Mistress, That Bitch Who Won't Stop Torturing me, The Love of My Life says "At the max time setting I'll come back to let you down sometime on Tuesday Slave"

She turns very slowly to leave and walks away slower then ever. I'm so glad she didn't put my blindfold back as the words run through my mind one more time "I hate to see you go but love to watch you leave"

Just then I feel more intense shocks to my still wet, my God! How is it still wet? Pussy. Between the tingling to my breasts, nipples, body, both inside and outside my Pussy and ass seems to grow quicker and more intense this time.

Why is it more intense so quick? I close my eyes, tip my head back as my stretched out helplessly bound, strapped and suspended body goes into a combination of shivers, shakes and uncontrollable orgasms that blend right into each other . . .

*"I wish to say Thank You Reader
for spending some of your Precious
Time with Me in my World"*
Love Zatanna

1

---

1. https://www.amazon.com/Zatanna-Dark/e/

B08RPCLY7M

*Feel Free to Contact Me with
Comments, Suggestions, Requests -
ZatannaXtraDark@Gmail.com
Twitter: @dark_zatanna*

Don't miss out!

Visit the website below and you can sign up to receive emails whenever Zatanna Dark publishes a new book. There's no charge and no obligation.

https://books2read.com/r/B-A-ARBLB-WUAID

BOOKS2READ

Connecting independent readers to independent writers.

Also by Zatanna Dark

BONDAGE BETA-TESTS

Bondage Beta-Tester - BDSM Enhancement Upgrade . . . Inevitable

Bondage Beta-Tested - BDSM Sassy Mistress Upgrade . . . Activated

BONUS BONDAGE AND THE HOLIDAYS

Final Bondage Easter - Bunny's Lap = Spanking & Eggs Gets You Keys

Final Bondage Valentine's - This Year Jill Is The Gift Given To Be Punished!

Final Bondage Xmas Eve - Don't Unrope Her Until Morning

Mother's Day Final Bondage - Time To Treat Herself To Spanking & BDSM

Latex Bondage Slave Rental

Final Bondage Slave Rental - Sexual Urges To Be Helplessly Punished Wins

Final Bondage Rental Blue - Unlimited Spanking of Latex Slave Is Included

Final Bondage Rental White - Leather Paddling Invites Unlimited Orgasms

STRANGER BONDAGES
Bound To A Stranger - A Dangerous Game of Betrayal
Revenge Of A Stranger - A Taste Of Her Own Medicine

Standalone
Final Bondage Hotel Surprise - Slave Needing a Spanking Include with Room
Anonymous Final Bondage - Unexpected Unknown Unrelenting
Final Bondage Hesitation - It's Painful Being Mistress's Newest Slave
Random Final Bondage - "No Safety-Net Rule"
Final Bondage Therapy - Torture, Tease or Spankings, Yes Please!
Final Bondage Interrogation - Flog Torture Tie Tease Whip . . . Repeat
Final Bondage Threesome - Mistress Loves Spanking, Teasing, Denying & CBT
Final Bondage Audition - They'll Do Anything to Get the Part
Final Steampunk Bondage - Steam Powered Spanking Machine
Final Bondage Magic - Straight Jacket Spanking? Yes Please!
Final Couples Bondage - Punished & Spanked for No Reason
Final Bondage Safe Room - Bound Helpless and Hidden Forever
Final Bondage Delivered - B-day Six-Pack: Spanking Paddling Cropping Cat-O-Nine Caning & Whipping
Final Bondage Wish Granted - Careful What You Wish For
Final Bondage Hotel - Mistress of Tease & Denial Puts Me On Hold
Final Bondage Revenge Blue - He Doesn't Believe in Hard Limits, Big Mistake!
Final Bondage Surprise - It's Permanent Mummification!
Finally In Bondage Vegas - You Won The Karma Slot Machine!
Final Bondage Giggles Revenge - She Couldn't Be Happier To Play Your Games

Final Bondage Beta-Test - Helplessly Torture Tie Tease & Spankings
Final Bondage Writer - Writing Your Own BDSM Story Makes It
Reality
Final Bondage Tag-Team - Earning Their Way Out Of Male Chastity
Final Self Bondage Auction - She Won You And Has Decided Your Fate
Final Self Bondage - Do You Promise Me You're Helpless?
Spring Break Final Bondage - Princess Tease Deserves Her Spanking
Final Bondage Spoiled - Mistress Doesn't Care What The Rich Girl
Slave Wants
Red Light Blue Light - Some Games You Never Grow Out Of
Final Backstage Bondage - Here Cums the Understudy
Final Bondage Workout - Mistress of Tease & Denial, CBT and Edging
Final Ultra-Doll Bondage - Your Ultimate BDSM Dominatrix
Final Babysitter Bondage - Please Tease Me Punish Me Spank Me
Bondage Beta-Test 001 - Firewall Failure + Jealous Girlfriend =
Revenge
Final Bondage Mistress Contest - Winner Gets to Keep the Loser as
Her Slave
Final Bondage Volunteer - Today's Class: Spanking & Paddling
Final Bondage Twins - Her Freedom Traded for Permanent Slavery
Final Bondage Tied & Seek - U'R Their Toy to Spank Tease Punish
Final Bondage Playdate - CBT & Edging Are Her Favorite Ways To
Play
Final Bondage Paralytic

About the Author

Welcome to My World. I didn't start Truly Living in it myself until Experiencing My first moment of True Helplessness. As we walk the World Day to Day, there's Endless Responsibilities weighing us down. Taking away our Joy. Yes, you can try to enjoy the Day, but what about taking care of this or doing that. Maybe you should be doing all of those things instead of Fully Enjoying your Day . . .Or, we could go to the Bar, do some Drugs, trying to just Relax. Trust me, this doesn't work. The moment you've finally taken enough to Relax, to just forget about your worries, is also the same moment your Senses are so Dulled, you miss or forget the Pleasure. There was your chance to bring back your Joy . . . too bad you won't remember it.Imagine with me a Different and Way Better Option. Imaging the moment where none of your other Endless Responsibilities matter. They just don't matter because even if you wanted to work on them, you can't. There's no Guilt here. When the choice of enjoying every Second of Pleasure becomes Your Only Choice. Now imagine this with all of your Senses Heightened as the Memory of this moment stays with you Long After . . .I'm sharing with my True reasons for enjoying Bondage. To be Tied Helplessly. To Tie Another Helplessly. To be Bound naked Breasts to Breasts while Helpless. To share my Stories of the Helpless with you, My Much Loved Reader. As you can see the Common word is Helpless. Let me explain why you Must be Helpless for the Pleasure to Fully take over your Body, Soul and Mind.For your Mind to Fully enter the World of Pure Pleasure you must first be completely Un-Bound from your Endless Responsibilities. As long as the choice to work on them exists, you will Never be Free of them, not even for a moment. This can Only Happen once you're Completely, Totally, Utterly Helpless. If you can Houdini your way loose, if you can talk your way out, if you can just use your Puppy Dog Eyes and Sad face to be release, Then You Were Never Helpless.WARNING: Many of my Stories involved No Safe-Word, Not knowing your Safe-Word, being Gagged and unable to say your Safe-Word. This can and is Very Dangerous, as you'll learn through the eyes of some of my Characters. For myself, my Characters and you seeing through their eyes, this takes the overall experience, pain & pleasure to the Next Level.

Read more at https://www.amazon.com/Zatanna-Dark/e/B08RPCLY7M.